ROTTEN RALPH'S
Rotten Family

Written by **Jack Gantos**

Illustrated by **Nicole Rubel**

Farrar Straus Giroux

New York

For Mabel and Grace —J.G.

For my family —N.R.

Farrar Straus Giroux Books for Young Readers
175 Fifth Avenue, New York 10010

Color separations by Bright Arts (H.K.) Ltd.
Printed in China by South China Printing Co. Ltd.,
Dongguan City, Guangdong Province
Designed by Jay Colvin
First edition, 2014
1 3 5 7 9 10 8 6 4 2

mackids.com

Library of Congress Cataloging-in-Publication Data
Gantos, Jack.
  Rotten Ralph's rotten family / written by Jack Gantos ; illustrated by Nicole
Rubel. — First edition.
      pages cm
  Summary: "Ralph takes a swing through his family tree to find out why he's
so rotten"—Provided by publisher.
  ISBN 978-0-374-36353-6 (hardback)
  [1. Cats—Fiction.   2. Behavior—Fiction.   3. Families—Fiction.]   I. Rubel,
Nicole, illustrator.   II. Title.

PZ7.G15334Roki 2014
[E]—dc23
                                                                    2013022076

Farrar Straus Giroux Books for Young Readers may be purchased for
business or promotional use. For information on bulk purchases please
contact Macmillan Corporate and Premium Sales Department
at (800) 221-7945 x5442 or by email at specialmarkets@macmillan.com.

The character of Rotten Ralph was originally created by
Jack Gantos and Nicole Rubel.

Contents

Born to Be Me

Ralph was Sarah's rotten cat and Sarah loved him from the moment she brought him home.

But one evening Sarah hung up the telephone and sighed.

"That's it, Ralph," she said, holding up a list and crossing off the last name. "There is not a cat sitter in town who will watch you for one night. Now I won't be able to go to the birthday party sleepover."

Rotten Ralph smiled. He knew why Sarah couldn't get a sitter. He pushed one of them too hard on the backyard swing. She flew over the fence and into the neighbor's pool. He taught the next one how to hypnotize his pet snake. She left cross-eyed.

He used the last sitter's makeup for
Halloween practice. She ran off in a
snit.

"Word has gotten around," said
Sarah, "that you are way too rotten!"

About time! Ralph said to himself. I
don't need a babysitter.

I can stay home by myself, he thought gleefully. He had a lot of new rotten ideas to try.

But Sarah read his sneaky mind. "Oh no," she said. "The last time you stayed home alone you tied yourself to the ceiling fan."

Ralph grinned. He liked that one.

"Where did you learn to be so rotten?" Sarah asked.

Ralph shrugged. He had never given it much thought, since he had always been rotten.

"Well, things are going to change," Sarah declared. "From now on, you better be on your best behavior!"

Rotten Ralph yawned.

"Since you are so tired," said Sarah, "you can just march up to your room and think long and hard about why you are so rotten."

Sarah went to her room, too. "I'll just stay home and read," she said. She tried to open her book, but Ralph had glued all the pages together with peanut butter. She threw her hands up into the air. "There better be some changes in the morning . . . or else!"

Rotten Family Tree

Rotten Ralph sat on his bed. "I'm in trouble again," he muttered, and leafed through a photo album of his family.

He flipped to a photograph of his sweet mother. "So why am I so rotten?" he wondered. "My mother always let me do anything I wanted." He missed her.

"Those were the good old days," he sighed, "when I didn't have to change a thing about myself."

He turned to some baby pictures.

"Look how cute I am at feeding time,"
he purred. "What could have gone
wrong?"

"And Father loved changing my
diapers," he remembered with a smile.
"He never once said that I smelled
rotten."

At his first birthday party Ralph did not share his cake. He ate it all.

"Nothing wrong with that," he said. "Only *my* name was written on it."

And he showed his younger brother and sister how to play well with others.

They looked up to me, he thought proudly.

As he grew a little older he had to help out around the house. When it was Ralph's turn to wash the dishes he always felt sleepy.

"Everyone knows a nap after dinner is the best," he said.

Ralph's aunt Eva von Rotten loved to paint.

So did Ralph. He helped her improve her pictures.

"She always treasured my advice and thanked me for it."

Once a week, on laundry day, he helped his grandmother get clean. "She liked it when I scrubbed behind her ears," he recalled.

At bedtime his grandfather read him
a story. Ralph loved to act out the rotten
parts. I learned so much from books, he
thought.

"Maybe Sarah wouldn't think I was so rotten if she didn't have so many rules around the house," he said to himself.

He flipped back to the picture of his sweet mother. I wish I was with my family again, Ralph thought. They always did everything I wanted.

He slipped out the window and ran away into the dark, dark night. He ran all the way back to the family farm.

Swing Your Cat

Ralph arrived way past bedtime, but his whole family was still wide awake.

His mother greeted him at the door. "My mischievous little kitten!" She led him into the kitchen and gave him a healthy helping of shoe stew. "What brings you back home?"

"I'm wondering why I'm so rotten," Ralph asked.

"You were never rotten to me," she replied. "Go ask your father. But be careful."

His father was in the barnyard milking the goat. "What are you doing back home?" he asked.

"I've come to find out why I am so rotten."

His father squirted him in the eye with goat's milk. "I don't know, son," he replied. "After you feed those pigs you can go ask your brother and sister."

After Ralph fed the pigs he needed a little catnap. When he woke up he was missing some fur.

"Aren't you proud?" said his brother and sister, who were shearing sheep. "We grew up to be rotten just like you!"

His mother came to the rescue. "Don't pick on poor Ralphie," she said. "He has always been so delicate."

Rotten Ralph loved his mother.

"Now go upstairs to visit your aunt and uncle," she said.

"What are you doing back here?"
asked Uncle Claws.

"I was wondering where I learned
how to be so rotten?" Ralph asked.

"I have no idea," Uncle Claws replied.
Then he sat on his nephew until Ralph
cried "Uncle!"

His aunt Eva von Rotten rolled Ralph
into a giant ball of yarn and bounced
him down the stairs.

"Momma!" Ralph yelled.

His mother caught him. "That must
have been an accident," she said. "Aunt
von Rotten has always been so gentle."

Ralph took a deep breath and went to see his sweet grandmother.

"I've been waiting for you to return," she said, and pointed to a mountain of dirty, stinking socks. "I've saved these for you to wash."

She smiled as Ralph scrubbed.

"I have a question," Ralph said to his grandfather, who asked Ralph to brand a bull. The bull tossed Ralph into a tree.

"Did you have a question, sonny?" his grandfather asked.

"Never mind," Ralph said. He already knew the answer.

Seeing my family has been no fun, Ralph thought. Before the night was over he decided it was time to leave.

When he kissed his mother goodbye, she saw a tear in Ralph's eye. "Did you find out why you are so rotten?"

"Yes," said Ralph. "Because everyone was so rotten to me."

"Well, now it's time to be better than they are," she said. She wiped his eye and gave him a jug of shoe stew for the journey. "Go home to Sarah. You don't want her to worry."

Home Sweet Home

Being with Sarah is better than I ever knew, Ralph thought as he ran home in the dark. I never had it so good.

Sarah was still asleep when he climbed in his bedroom window. But Ralph didn't go to sleep. He was going to make some changes of his own.

He cleaned up his room. He put away
his toys. He threw away all his junk.
He even cleaned the fish tank without
eating the fish.

Then he tiptoed downstairs. He washed his scribbles off the wall. He fluffed up the sofa pillows. He cleaned the rugs. He put his pet lizards back into their cage.

The sun was rising when Ralph tied on an apron and got ready to cook.

In the kitchen he squeezed oranges
for juice and whipped up a pitcher of
hot chocolate.

He made special pancakes with maple syrup. He put flowers in a vase and everything on a tray.

Then he served Sarah breakfast in
bed.

She was very surprised. "I don't know
what brought about this change," said
Sarah, "but I love it."

Ralph remembered his sweet mother.
She always believed I would turn out
to be a very good cat, he thought with a
smile.

When Sarah finished her breakfast
Rotten Ralph jumped up onto her lap.

"It's so nice to curl up at home with
my sweet little Ralphie," said Sarah.

Yes, thought Ralph. Where I can do
anything I want. Then he closed his
eyes and purred his happy purr.